D0284612

Read more of Finn Caspian's

alien adventures!

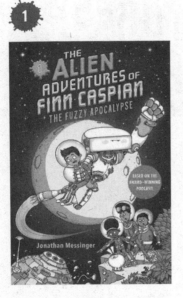

THE ALIEN ADVENTURES OF FINN CASPIAN

THE FUZZY APOCALYPSE

Jonathan Messinger

Illustrated by Aleksei Bitskoff

HARPER

An Imprint of HarperCollinsPublishers

The Alien Adventures of Finn Caspian #1: The Fuzzy Apocalypse
Text copyright © 2020 by Jonathan Messinger
Illustrations copyright © 2020 by HarperCollins Publishers
Illustrations by Aleksei Bitskoff
All rights reserved. Printed in the United States of America.
No part of this book may be used or reproduced in any manner
whatsoever without written permission except in the case of
brief quotations embodied in critical articles and reviews. For
information address HarperCollins Children's Books, a division of
HarperCollins Publishers, 195 Broadway, New York, NY 10007.
www.harpercollinschildrens.com

Library of Congress Control Number: 2020934464
ISBN 978-0-06-293215-0 — ISBN 978-0-06-293214-3 (pbk.)

Typography by Jessie Gang
20 21 22 23 24   PC/LSCH   10 9 8 7 6 5 4 3 2
❖
First Edition

For my men of adventure,

Griffin and Emerson

CONTENTS

A Note About This Story

The tale you are about to read takes place approximately **36.54372 million miles away** from Earth, as the crow flies. It has been collected and woven together via various interview transcripts, recordings, and interstellar **laser screams** sent to Earth from the *Famous Marlowe 280 Interplanetary Exploratory Space Station* over the past decade.

"Laser scream" may be a new term for you, as it is still not well understood on Earth, but we don't have time to get into it here.

The astronauts who boarded the *Marlowe* were charged with **one mission: to discover a planet where humans could one day live**. Captain Isabel Caspian sends out teams of explorers. Finn and his friends are all remarkable, but Finn will always have a special place in the history books.

Because Finn was the first kid born in space.

So in many ways, Finn was born for exactly the type of situation in which we find him here in this book. But it will be up to you to decide if that makes him lucky or not.

HALL OF EXPLORERS

Abigail Obaro

Troop 301 Captain

Finn Caspian

Chief Detective

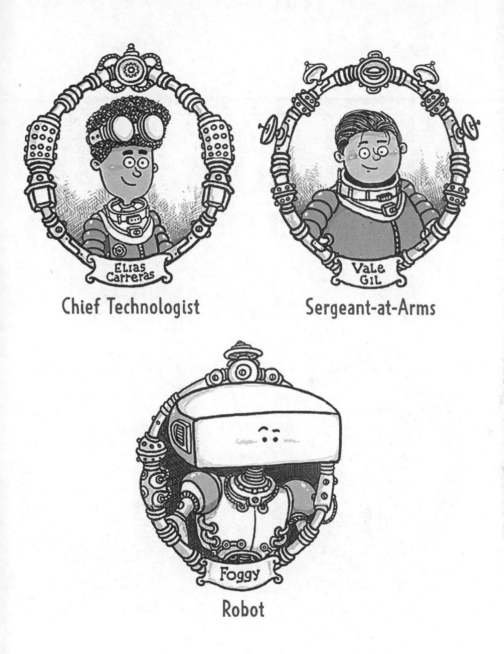

Chief Technologist

Sergeant-at-Arms

Robot

Chapter One
On the Clock

"Thank you so much for agreeing to stop our planet from exploding. You have seventeen minutes. Step right this way, please."

Finn Caspian looked at his best friend, Abigail Obaro. Besides being his best friend, she was captain of Explorers Troop 301. He wanted to make sure she was hearing the same thing he was. As far as he could tell, the aliens who were talking to them had no mouths. Their words seemed to just show up in his head. So he needed to make sure he wasn't imagining the whole planet-exploding thing.

He could see Abigail had heard it, too. She didn't say anything, but she reached up and twirled her finger around the outside of her space helmet as if she were twirling her dark, frizzy hair. It was the same thing she did anytime she got lost in thought. She looked confused and also up for a challenge, which was the mix of emotions that usually got them into the worst trouble.

"Let's go," shrugged Abigail.

Finn followed Abigail, and Abigail followed the little gray creatures. As the chief detective of Explorers Troop 301, Finn had seen plenty of aliens in his time. He'd seen extraterrestrials as big as planets, two-headed creatures, and aliens made of rock, ice, and lava, just to name a few. But these little beings were different.

They were short and gray, with four eyes and no mouths. They had large heads, which was common among aliens, but their skulls were all strangely translucent. It was like their heads were balloons someone had inflated just a bit too much, and you could see into them. Finn could barely make out the brains inside. They looked like glowing purple tennis balls with electric currents coursing through them.

"Watch your step." Finn nearly tripped on the step leading up to a cobblestone pathway. Again, the words had appeared in Finn's head. He noticed this time that the brains in the aliens' heads glowed brighter when they spoke.

He looked back at his friend Elias Carreras, who was playing with the walkie-talkie built into the sleeve of his space suit. The explorers used the walkie-talkies to keep in touch with the space station on their missions. Elias was the troop's chief technologist.

"I think this thing is on the fritz," he said. "I'll take it apart as soon as we're back on the *Marlowe*."

Okay, so he must have heard the same voices Finn had. Every time something went wrong, Elias tried to fix it with technology.

Finn stood on his toes to catch a glimpse of his oldest friend, Vale Gil, the troop's sergeant-at-arms, whose dark brown eyes seemed to be searching the sky for—

"Did he say this place is going to blow up?" yelled Vale. "Why are we still here? And how are they talking without mouths? It's like their words are in my brain. I got word brain! Am I going crazy?"

Finn never really had to read Vale's expressions to know what he was thinking.

The final member of Explorers Troop 301 to follow the little aliens was Foggy, Finn's robot. He looked as pleased as could be. Foggy had been on countless adventures with the troop, and they'd come to rely on his loyalty and his fearlessness. He was also strangely optimistic in the face of things like exploding planets.

"Oooohhh, stopping a planet from exploding should be impossible," said the robot. His voice, which Finn had once described as sounding like a hair dryer starting up, whistled through the planet's thin air. "Let's give it a try!"

The astronauts followed the aliens through an archway into a garden. They walked down a stone path surrounded by enormous plants. Giant flowers of all colors towered over the kids. It was like walking into a jungle, but with a pleasant path of cobblestone to follow. Finn felt like some of the plants were watching them. Their petals turned toward the kids as they walked by.

Typically, the *Marlowe*'s kid explorer troops

only visited planets that had already been scouted. The space station's scientists would scan the planet to see if it was dangerous. If they decided it was safe, the kids would go down and check it out. It was their version of school: rocket off to far-flung planets and study them. This time, however, Troop 301 had been headed toward a different planet, when something on this planet had lassoed their ship and dragged them down to its green surface.

"I still don't like that they took control of our pod," said Abigail, who always piloted their ship.

"Let's hope they don't take control of our brains, too," said Finn.

"Hahahahaha," the aliens laughed. "We can't control your brains. Only speak directly to them. Sixteen minutes until the explosion, by the way! Please hurry."

The kids ducked under the low branches of a tree and came out the other side into a large atrium. Three giant gray aliens stood waiting for them.

Finn didn't like the look of these aliens. While the ones they'd first met had seemed harmless enough, something about these giants was more menacing. They had four eyes like the others, but big, gaping mouths, too. And they nervously shuffled their feet as if they were going to charge like rhinos.

"Let me guess," said Vale. "These are the guys who are going to destroy your planet in sixteen minutes."

"Fifteen minutes now." The tiny aliens' brains all glowed bright purple. "And no, these are simply the—"

"Fifteen?!" one of the massive aliens boomed. It leapt in fright, and all three of the giants started running—straight at the explorers.

Chapter Two
A Robot, a Dream, and a Spitball

Finn, Abigail, Elias, and Vale were not just an explorer troop: they were also best friends. They had been since they were little, when they'd play hide-and-seek on the captain's bridge. Finn and Abigail liked to hide in the *Marlowe*'s map room. Elias would sneak into the robot room to watch the engineers work.

Vale would look all over for them, armed with a straw full of spitballs.

As they got older, their parents saw that the four of them were a great team and put them together into Explorers Troop 301. They began training to explore the galaxy. Finn discovered that his love of puzzles could serve him well on an alien planet. Elias got to tinker with robots, and Vale discovered a love of battles. (Well, simulated battles, like video games. He wasn't quite as brave on strange planets.)

It was clear from the start that Abigail was their leader. She had the most courage, she had the most sense, and, unlike her friends, she could make a decision in less than twenty minutes.

The four of them trained for hours together on the *Marlowe*. When they weren't practicing, they were playing practical jokes on each other (like the time Vale filled Finn's space helmet with mint jelly and told him it was alien slime).

The biggest day for a kid on the *Marlowe*, though, was their eighth birthday, when they got their very own robot. Troop 301 hadn't been complete until Finn's eighth birthday, when he got a robot built especially for him: Foggy. Elias had helped his parents build Foggy, pulling the design from his overstuffed notebook of robot drawings.

Foggy wasn't a high-speed, high-tech robot with laser cannons and supersonic jets. In fact, his head looked like a wedge of cheese balanced on top of a pencil. But he had something hardwired into him, something that no amount of plug-ins or add-ons could give him. Foggy had a love of adventure. Which was probably why, when those three giant

aliens charged at the kids and the four of them got ready to scatter, Foggy yelled, "Tallyho!" and flew straight at the monsters.

It wasn't his best idea.

Chapter Three
I'm Going to Need You to Spell That

"Foggy, up!" Abigail shouted. "Grab us and go!"

Maybe Foggy only heard the first part. The stomping of the giant gray aliens was so loud Abigail could hardly hear herself. As soon as the aliens started charging the kids, Foggy activated the rocket boosters in his feet. He shot off directly toward the giants as Finn, Abigail, Elias, and Vale scattered behind him.

To be fair to Foggy, he did catch the giants by surprise. They didn't know what to do with this strange metal creature flying straight at them. The giant in the middle stopped dead in its tracks and cocked its head to the side.

Maybe it was the fire coming out of Foggy's feet. Maybe it was the fact that Foggy had been standing still a second ago and was now shooting directly at it. Or maybe it was the big smile on Foggy's face as he flew straight at the giant's nose.

"Hallo, friend!" cried Foggy just before the middle giant swatted him away. Foggy bounced off the belly of the alien on the right, then off the belly of the alien on the left, and finally came to a clumsy halt on the floor.

"Well, that was unpleasant," said the robot. "And I believe we have eleven minutes and forty-two seconds now to solve your little—"

Foggy held up his hand to the giants.

"DON'T run around screaming or smack me again, big things," Foggy said. "I'm simply stating, we need to get to work."

In the back of the courtyard, the four explorers were hiding behind a stem of giant berries that dangled off one of the plants.

"Okay," Vale whispered to his friends. "Abigail and Finn, you two climb this plant. Elias and I will pass you this bunch of berries here. When you get to the top, throw them at the giants. See if you can splatter them on their faces so they can't see. Then Elias and I will run out of the garden and meet you two and Foggy back at the explorer pod. Got it?"

"So your plan is that Abigail and I throw a bunch of fruit at three angry giants while you two slip away?" said Finn. He was starting to sweat from the heat of the gardens. The fact that his thick black hair had stuck to his forehead was only adding to his frustration. There's no good way to get sweaty hair out of your eyes with an eight-pound helmet on your head. "That sounds like a great plan if your name isn't Abigail or Finn."

"Yeah," said Abigail. "And there are only eight berries in this bunch, but there are three aliens with four eyes each, so that's twelve. Maybe while we're throwing berries at them, you two can run out and poke the other four eyes."

"Ha-ha, very funny," said Vale. "Got any

other ideas? Those three are going to blow up this planet in a couple minutes, so make it snappy."

"STOP!" Another alien voice, louder than the other ones, rang out in the explorers' heads. "My guards are a little jumpy, but they would never harm this planet."

"How about four kids and a tin can?" asked Vale. "They have any plans to harm us?"

But the giant aliens were already shuffling back between the tall trees. Something had spooked them. A small alien walked out from the shadows. It looked like the smaller aliens that had met the explorers when they landed, only its tennis-ball brain shone bright red.

There was also something about the look on its face, the openness of its four eyes, that helped the explorers relax. They made their way out from under the leaves, embarrassed to have cowered in the corner. Finn helped Foggy off the ground.

"You okay?" Finn whispered.

"Never better," said Foggy.

"You just got smacked by a giant and bounced off two bellies," said Finn. "You sure about that?"

"Of course!" said Foggy. "I think the little red-brained guy is about to send us on our adventure."

The explorers all felt the alien leader laugh.

"Correct. My name is GARKROFAFWP-BALOW."

That's the best way to write the word the alien said. It actually sounded like three wolves howling, one car crashing into glass, and four grasshoppers chirping, all at the same time.

"Ow," said Elias. "That's your name?"

"Yes. I'm sorry—as you can see by the color in my head, I have been unwell lately. It is hard for me to translate my thoughts into your language. And towing your ship to our planet took a lot of my energy. Please, you can call me—"

"Don't say it again!" said Vale, covering his ears.

"Doug," said the alien.

"Much better," said Abigail.

"Doug is our elder," said the chorus of small aliens. They had been quiet since leading the explorers into the garden. "This entire planet has existed for centuries because Doug has been all-powerful. He brought us together, fended off enemies, and cared for the luscious gardens you see all around. All hail Doug. Doug the Magnificent. Doug the Wonderful. Doug the—"

"Got it," said Vale. "Doug's the Dougiest. How much time do we have left?"

"Eight minutes and forty-one seconds," said Doug.

They all looked at the giants, who seemed like they were going to jump out of their skin.

"Operating this planet has been the joy of my life," said Doug. "But now we have an enemy here who is destroying it. An enemy so fierce and so fast, I cannot stop it, nor even keep up with it."

"Have you sent any of the big guys after it?" Finn asked.

"I have sent dozens. Only three remain," said Doug. He was quiet for a moment.

"Okay," said Abigail. "We're here. We'll give you five minutes before we need to be back on our pod and out of here. So point us in the right direction, and we'll see what we can do."

"Here, here!" said Foggy. "What is it and how do we stop it?"

"It is a loathsome, fearsome creature," said Doug. "It is eating our entire planet. And right now, yes, I can sense it, it is headed for your ship."

Chapter Four
Family Photos

"Foggy, fly us to the ship, *now*!" said Abigail. She burst out of the aliens' gardens and paused to let the robot pick her up.

"Hold on," said Finn. "We don't know what we're facing, and we don't know how we're going to stop it. If we go charging in there right now, we may not have a chance."

"We have about eight minutes of chances,

anyway," said Abigail. "Either we go right now or we blow up with the planet."

"I just think we should wait a second and come up with a plan first," said Finn.

"I'm the captain, Finn," said Abigail. "We don't have time to argue."

"Well, I'm the oldest, so . . . ," said Finn.

"So that just makes you old," said Abigail.

Finn was surprised. The "I'm the oldest" trick had won him so many arguments when picking capture-the-flag teams back on the *Marlowe*.

"Kids, let's not argue," said Foggy. He followed Finn and Abigail out, and the aliens trailed behind them.

"There is no argument, since I'm captain," said Abigail.

"Fine," said Finn. But you didn't need a glowing brain to see that everything was not fine.

"Doug!" said Foggy, pretending like Finn and Abigail weren't staring each other down. "Great and wondrous Doug. Since you can put words in our heads, are you also able to place pictures?"

"Doug can do anything!" all of the explorers heard at once.

"You want to see the beast before you face it?" said Doug. "You are wise, metal man. Yes, one moment."

Doug's head glowed bright red, lighting up the underside of the trees. A clear picture formed in the explorers' minds, like a memory. The enemy looked just like Doug, but its brain glowed yellow, and it wore an elaborate headdress, like a hat with vines that stretched toward the sky.

"You want us to stop this thing?" said Elias. "Why do you need us? It looks just like you all."

"Oh, wait! Sorry," said Doug. "That is a picture of my sister. Hold on, let me transmit the right photo."

The explorers suddenly saw photos of Doug's children as babies. Then they saw a scene at the beach where Doug had something that looked like an angry crab latched on to his toe. And then they saw Doug as a child burying his pet slug in his backyard.

"Doug," said Finn. "This is starting to feel a little uncomfortable."

"Oh, sorry! I can't seem to find the right—aha! Here it is, sending you the picture now."

"We don't have time for this," said Abigail.

"I don't know, it seems important to me," said Finn.

A new image entered the explorers' minds. But all they were seeing was a small furry creature.

"Are you sure this is it?" said Vale. "It's really small."

"Yes," said Doug.

"And furry?" said Elias.

"Affirmative," said Doug.

"And it has floppy ears," said Abigail.

"The floppiest," said Doug.

"And really cute little toes," said Finn.

"Just the cutest!" said Doug.

"So we have to ask, then," said Foggy. "Great and wondrous Doug: Why are you so afraid of this little creature? And  how could a bunny possibly blow up an entire planet?"

"Do not be fooled by its appearance," said Doug. "Many have made that mistake before. It will end all life on this planet in a matter of five minutes and forty-five seconds. So please hurry."

"Okay," said Abigail, "all in favor of stopping this little death bunny and then getting back to the *Marlowe* before supper?"

All the explorers raised their hands. They each grabbed on to Foggy as the robot blasted away from the planet's surface.

"So long, beautiful Doug!" yelled Foggy. "We will not fail you."

"Try not to die, friends," they all heard Doug say as they flew away. "You very probably will!"

The explorers felt a chill run through them.

"Doug's the worst," said Vale.

Chapter Five
A Bunny Thing
Happened . . .

As the explorers approached their ship, everything looked just as they had left it. The door
remained closed. Nothing looked like it had
been moved or even touched in any way.

Finn was the first to spot the tracks on the
ground. Little paw prints came out of the nearby
forest and circled their explorer pod. Finn and

his friends looked around but couldn't see any sign of the bunny.

Finn punched the code into the panel on the side of the ship. The hatch opened.

"Aaaaaahhhhhhh!" A shriek sounded from inside.

All the explorers put their hands to their ears—even Foggy. The small, furry creature Doug had shown them was sitting in the pilot's seat. It had its fuzzy little paws on the controls. And apparently it was as scared of the explorers as they were of it, because its scream curled all their toes.

"Aaaaaahhhhhhh!"

"Please stop," said Finn. "We're not here to harm you."

The creature stared at Finn with large, frightened eyes. Its lower lip quivered, and its whole body seemed to vibrate in the pilot chair.

"Well, we might be here to harm it, if we're being honest," said Vale.

"Aaahhhhhhhh!" yelled the bunny creature.

"Wait, no!" said Abigail. "Ignore my friend. He has trouble understanding . . . everything."

"Hey!" said Vale. "I understood that!"

Abigail shook her head.

"We're not here to harm you," she said. "We're just here to stop you."

"Stop me from what?" the death bunny said. "Stealing your ship? I wasn't going to steal your ship. Why are you accusing me of trying to steal your ship?"

"No one's accusing you of anything," said Finn. "But you are sitting in the pilot's seat. And you are pushing the launch button over and over again."

Click, click, click. The bunny tapped at the big red button.

"Aaaaahhh . . . ," the rabbit screamed again, but its heart wasn't in it. The scream trailed off.

"Okay, fine, I was trying to steal your ship," said the bunny. "But that's only because this planet is going to explode in two minutes. I need to get out of here."

"We were told you were the one doing the exploding," said Abigail.

The explorers all studied the furry little creature carefully. It looked capable of nibbling a small patch of grass to death. But beyond that, it didn't look dangerous.

"Let me guess, the great and wondrous Doug told you I was going to do it," said the bunny. "That guy. Never trust someone who can literally put ideas in your head."

The bunny creature told the explorers that there were once thousands and thousands of species on the planet. It hadn't been paradise. There were predators and prey, and extreme weather. But it had been a fine planet, and many of the creatures lived peacefully together. Until Doug had decided that he and his kind were better than everyone else, and they began hunting other living things. They took over land that didn't belong to them and put ideas into the heads of the animals to get them to turn on each other.

"Pretty soon, it was just me and my kin, and Doug and his," said the bunny. "We swore we would never fight. So the rest of my family, and my kind, all evacuated the planet weeks ago."

"Everyone but me," the bunny continued. "I refused to leave. He's been after me ever since."

"So, what, he's blowing up the entire planet just to get you?" said Elias. "I can't believe he lied to us."

"Oh no, I'm definitely blowing up the planet," said the bunny. "If we can't have it, neither can he."

"I thought you said you weren't going to blow up the planet," said Finn.

"No, you all said that," said the bunny. "I just guessed that Doug told you my plans."

The explorers huddled outside their pod. They were split on who to trust, Doug or the death bunny.

"I mean, he kind of lied to us about blowing up the planet," said Finn.

"Yeah, but you heard what he said about Doug wiping out the other species," said

Abigail. "And he's right. You can't trust some-one who can put an idea in your head the way Doug can."

"But we can't trust someone who's trying to steal our ship, either," said Finn.

"But where is everyone else?" said Elias. "I think the death bunny is telling the truth. Maybe Doug just wants the planet for him-self."

"This is such a dumb planet," said Vale. "Why would anyone want it?"

"Well, as captain, I say we—" said Abigail.

"As second-in-command, I say we—" Finn interrupted.

"Guys," said Foggy, interrupting everyone. "We had five minutes and forty-five seconds when we left the gardens and now we only have—"

And the planet exploded.

Chapter Six
Fun Ways to Explode

Have you ever seen a
planet explode? There
are a ton of different
ways for it to happen.
There is the supernova,
where everything
blows apart and pieces
of the planet scatter millions

of light-years away. There is the implosion, where the planet collapses in on itself, as though squeezed in the fist of an invisible giant.

And there are the less common explosions, like the balloon, where a geyser of steam sends a deflating planet zooming across the cosmos. Or the banana, where each layer of the planet peels off and then an enormous galactic monkey eats it. Doug's planet suffered what scientists call a "coconut." The planet was split in two, a jagged fault line breaking across the globe like a crack in the sidewalk.

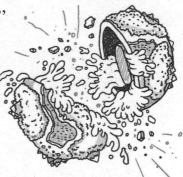

And that crack, ever widening, happened to be right where the explorers of Troop 301 had landed their explorer pod. Two sheer cliffs emerged. Abigail, Elias, and the bunny stood on one side. Finn, Vale, and Foggy were left on the other side, closer to Doug and his gardens.

"Foggy!" shouted Abigail. "The ship, it's going to fall into that crack!"

"I agree!" yelled Foggy.

"Good to hear!" said Abigail. "But could you please fly down and see if you can use your rockets to push it back up?"

"Of course!" Foggy dove into the ravine. The chasm was now almost as wide as the ship itself. The round pod was stuck in it like an M&M in a nostril. Foggy flew beneath it and put all his power into trying to lift it out, but it wouldn't budge.

"Foggy, can you get to the ship's controls and fly it out of there?!" shouted Abigail.

"No way," said Finn. "It's too dangerous. Foggy weighs too much. The ship will just sink even farther."

"Foggy, do it," said Abigail.

"Hey, don't tell my robot what to do," said Finn.

"Who is captain here again?" said the bunny, pointing a paw at Finn.

"Yeah, are you the captain now?" cried Abigail over the rumbling of the planet's slow explosion. "Are you giving orders?"

The explorer pod loosened and slipped deeper into the chasm.

"If I were, I wouldn't do something so—" said Finn. But he didn't finish the thought. He couldn't finish the thought. Suddenly, he forgot what he was going to say. Visions of Doug's children playing in the sand flickered through his head. A little baby alien was crying. Finn had a strange desire to change its little alien diaper. . . .

"Forget it!" yelled Finn, shaking his head. "If you're so smart, you two figure it out."

Finn and Vale high-fived and started walking toward Doug's compound.

"What was that all about?" said Elias.

"Doug," said the bunny. "They've been Doug'd."

Abigail was going to ask the bunny what he meant, but she got distracted by an enormous crashing sound. The chasm opened, and the explorer pod fell out of reach.

Their only way off this planet had just slipped toward the white-hot center of the planet.

"Finn?" said Abigail. But Finn was too far away to hear her.

"Are you guys always like this?" asked the bunny.

Chapter Seven
Doug in Control

Vale and Finn made their way back to Doug's gardens. They never for a moment wondered which way they should turn. It was like they could see a map drawn in their minds.

The supersized aliens stood guard. As Finn and Vale approached, the giants squatted down and pressed their shoulders together, forming an impenetrable wall.

Finn heard words form in his head.

"Let us pass, big ones," he said out loud. "Doug has sent for us." But the big ones didn't budge.

"AKLFJAFUOAIWFAFA!" Vale screamed at the giants in the aliens' native tongue. And the three oafs immediately bowed and stepped aside.

"What did I just say to them?" asked Vale.

"I don't know," said Finn. "You kind of sounded like an angry kitten."

A photo of Doug graduating from high school flickered into Finn's brain.

"I think something weird is going on," Finn whispered to Vale. "Do you keep—"

"Well, that didn't work!" yelled Doug. He and the other small aliens emerged from a path up ahead. "I thought you could stop the planet from blowing up, but nope! It has most definitely blown up. By my measure we have—"

Doug stopped himself. He looked over at the nervous giants by the gate and switched to a whisper.

"By my measure, we have about ten minutes until the whole planet is completely coconutted."

"What does that mean?" asked Vale.

The image of a planet appeared in Finn's and Vale's minds. The planet was cracked in half and opened up. The two sides floated away from each other. The molten rock on the inside of the planet spilled out, like the juice of, well, a coconut.

"Whoa," said Vale.

"Completely coconutted," said Doug. "But don't mention it in front of the big guys. I can barely keep them restrained as it is."

"Why are we here?" said Finn. "We should be helping our friends."

"They're not your friends," said Doug. "I heard you arguing with that Abigail. You're right; you're older than she is."

"They are our friends," said Finn. "Friends can argue. And wait, how did you hear me?"

"Um," said Doug. "AFJLAWEFJLAWFBE-AGI?!"

Finn had no idea what Doug just howled. But he thought he knew what he meant.

"Okay, you know what, we don't have time for this," said Doug. "Did I control your minds? Yes. But I don't like that term. I prefer to say you've been Doug'd."

"Get out of my head, man!" yelled Vale, smacking the side of his helmet like there was water in his ear.

"And you chose us because I was fighting with Abigail?" said Finn. He began to feel sick.

"Yes," said Doug. "You two were easy. You were already fighting with them. I just steered you in a different direction."

"No way," said Vale. "I don't believe you. You can't control our minds."

"I'm doing it right now," said Doug.

"No way," Vale repeated.

"Bark like a dog," said Doug.

"Woof," said Vale.

"See?" said Doug.

Finn tried to focus. He wanted to keep Doug out of his head. He looked down and saw that Doug and the other aliens were carrying suitcases.

"Yes," said Doug. "It is time for us to go now. All we have to do is make our way to your ship and we'll be off. I know a tropical planet just a few light-years from here where the beaches are gorgeous. So long as you can avoid the crabs . . . but never mind, let's go."

"You want to fly out in our ship?" said Vale.

"Of course!" said Doug. "That creature you

met, the one who banana'd our planet? Its family stole all our ships when they left. So now let's go. We need to get to your little pod."

"Banana'd?" said Finn. "I thought you said the planet coco—"

"It doesn't matter!" yelled Doug. His brain flashed a brilliant red. Finn's head suddenly hurt. It was like a siren went off in his mind. "We have to go now."

Finn looked at Vale, who was stooped over, covering his ears.

"You okay, Vale?"

"Yes, he's fine," said Doug. "He's fine, you're fine, we're all fine. And we're all going to fly out of here, right?"

Finn wasn't sure. But then he saw an image of him and the aliens flying away from the planet, laughing and sipping lemonade. The lemonade tasted like heaven. Vale must have

seen it, too, because he stood up straight and
began walking out of the gardens—straight for
their ship!

"AOFIUAFKLEFMLKAFN!" shouted Vale,
and the enormous guards parted, letting them
all pass.

Chapter Eight
Meanwhile, Back at the Crack

Abigail didn't know what to do. She was captain of the troop, but this was the first time she'd really had to make an important decision. Not only did she have to save her friends, there was an entire planet at stake.

"Okay, you two climb on my back," said the bunny. "We'll hop down to your ship and get out of here. I know it sounds dangerous, but I see some footholds on the cliff. And if you don't mind the smell of sizzling rabbit hair, I think we can make it down before we're all fried by the magma."

"Absolutely not," said Foggy. "It's too dangerous. Abigail, I really think we should go find Finn and Vale. It's not safe for us to split up like this."

Abigail kicked at the dirt. She had to take charge.

"You're right, Foggy," she said, snapping out of it. "You go find Finn and Vale and bring them back here. Elias, you start thinking of how we're going to get the ship out of the ravine and off this planet. Go! Quickly!"

Foggy rocketed off in search of his friends.

"Okay, Elias, what have you got for me?" said Abigail. "Um . . . Elias?"

Abigail turned around. Elias had run over to the edge of the forest and was hanging from the branch of a dead tree.

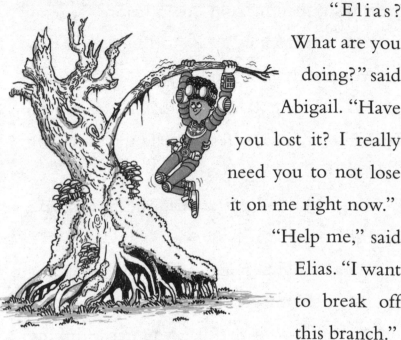

"Elias? What are you doing?" said Abigail. "Have you lost it? I really need you to not lose it on me right now."

"Help me," said Elias. "I want to break off this branch."

The bunny hopped over to Elias and grabbed hold of the branch. He kicked at the tree's trunk until the branch snapped off. The two of them fell to the ground.

"Great!" said Elias. "Okay, Bunny, can

you please break off another . . . hmmmm . . . seventy-three branches?"

"Sure," said the bunny. "How did you know I was a lumberjack?"

"Oh, I didn't," said Elias. "But that's great that you are because—"

"I'm not a lumberjack! That was a joke!" shouted the bunny. "Why are we doing arts and crafts? We need to get off this planet!"

Elias lifted the broken branch off the ground.

"It's not arts and crafts," said Elias. "It's engineering. When I get nervous, I make stuff. And I'm really nervous right now, so I'm going to make something big. Something that's going to get us off this planet."

Before the bunny or Abigail could ask what Elias had in mind, Foggy returned.

"I found Finn and Vale," said Foggy. If he weren't a robot, he would have been out of breath. "They're walking this way from Doug's. I asked them if they wanted me to fly them here, and Vale screamed something I couldn't understand."

"What?!" said Abigail. "Did you tell them we need their help?"

"I did, and Finn said, 'Buzz off, buckethead,'" said Foggy. "That I could understand."

"Go back to them and tell them you need them to fly here now," said Abigail. "Tell them Captain Abigail said so. It's an order."

Foggy nodded and jetted off.

"Now, Elias," said Abigail. "What do you have in mind with all these—"

Foggy returned.

"And?" said Abigail.

"One of those big aliens swatted at me," said Foggy. "Knocked me right back here. It was fun! I've never flown so fast!"

"Finn and Vale are staying with the aliens?" asked Elias. "That's not logical."

"Oh, this is not good," said the bunny. "We need to get out of here. If we're here when they get back, Doug will just take over all our brains, and that'll be it. He and his family will fly off, and we'll be left here on this dying coconut."

"Coconut? What are you talking about?" said Elias.

"Who knows," said Abigail. "Who knows what anyone on this planet is talking about."

"Abigail, perhaps if I flew you over to Finn, you could speak some sense to him?" said Foggy.

"No, forget it," said Abigail. "If he doesn't want to come to us, then we don't need him."

Abigail took a deep breath.

"Elias, Bunny, Foggy, let's get into those woods over there. Bunny, you can start pulling down branches for Elias's thingamajiggy. Elias, you can start building that thingamajiggy. Foggy, you and I will stay on the edge of the forest and spy on Finn and Doug to see what they're doing."

"I do not like this idea," said the bunny. "I like the idea where we get into your ship and fly away and forget about this whole thing."

"Too bad," said Abigail. "I give the orders. I'm the captain, whether anyone likes it or not."

Chapter Nine
Nobody Loves You When You're Down and Doug'd

Walking toward the chasm, Finn felt sick to his stomach. He didn't know why he was so annoyed with Foggy. Foggy was his robot! His best friend! But each time Foggy had flown over to convince him to talk with Abigail, something had itched at him. He couldn't explain it, but he felt angry, like Foggy was getting in the way.

He felt like he was *literally* seeing red whenever Foggy appeared.

He tried to remember something Doug had said about being Doug'd, but it was all a blur.

Vale was acting the same way. In fact, Vale didn't even seem like Vale anymore. The second time Foggy flew over to them, Vale laughed when the big alien swatted the robot.

Finn knew that wasn't right, but he also felt helpless.

"Don't worry, young explorers," said Doug. He was riding on the shoulder of one of the giants. "I know it is difficult to break away from one's friends. Living with others can be difficult. Leaders before me sought to build bridges between us and the other species on this planet. But building bridges takes a lot of work. Only I, Doug—"

"Doug!" shouted the other aliens.

"Yes, Doug. I knew that we needed to think only about ourselves. Since slowly removing the others from the planet, our kind has flourished. And if it weren't for that one annoying little bunny, we would have lived on for centuries here, happy and peaceful."

Something about Doug's speech seemed wrong to Finn, but he was having trouble clearing his thoughts.

"You can't just tell everyone what to do," said Finn.

"But that's my thing," said Doug.

"Yeah, but," Finn said. He tried to focus. "Just because you're the leader, that doesn't mean you get to decide everything. You should care what other people say. Like Abigail. She thinks just because she's captain—"

"Are you questioning Doug?" asked Doug.

"Doug!" cried the other aliens.

"No," said Finn.

The giant walking in front of Finn looked over his shoulder and growled.

"Good leaders respect their team," said Finn.

"It didn't seem like you were respecting Abigail," said Doug.

"I don't know," said Finn. "I guess you're right. Maybe I was wrong about Abigail. She wasn't trying to hurt us or anything. And she does listen sometimes—"

"Listen?" said Doug. "I have no need for that. For I am Doug."

"Doug!" shouted the other aliens.

"We have seven and a half minutes to get off this planet," said Doug. "Stop thinking about this Abigail. You're with me now."

And Finn, still feeling sick to his stomach, couldn't argue. For some reason, all he could think about was flying off in the explorer pod, drinking that lemonade, and sitting on a sandy beach.

Chapter Ten
A Robot and His Feelings

"Okay, here they come," said Abigail. She and Foggy had climbed a tree about fifteen feet from the ravine. Elias and the bunny were back in a clearing, working on Elias's invention.

It was getting dire now. The crack in the planet had opened even wider, and the rumbling made it difficult to hear anyone. Smoke rose off the branches of the trees closest to where the planet had split. The heat rising from the lava was making them dizzy.

"It's too smoky. I can't see what they're doing," said Abigail. "Can you make it out, Foggy?"

"Yes, I can see through the smoke," said the robot. "It appears they are approaching the edge of the chasm. It is Doug, three of the smaller aliens, and three of the large aliens. Finn and Vale are with them. And—Oh no."

The wind blew the smoke in a different direction, and Abigail strained her eyes to see why Foggy was upset. The problem was immediately clear. And horrifying. Vale's helmet was glowing with a bright-red light. She could make out a bit of light coming from Finn's, as well. But Finn's light was duller than Vale's and seemed to flicker.

"Does that mean what I think it means?"

asked Abigail, not really wanting to know.

"I'm afraid so," said Foggy. "It looks like
Doug has taken control of Finn's and Vale's
minds. No wonder Vale was speaking their
language. And now I know why Finn didn't
care when that brute smacked me away."

Abigail put her hand on Foggy's shoulder.

"I'm sure he was upset," said Abigail. "Finn would never let anyone hurt you. No matter what Doug has done—"

"Thank you, Abigail," said Foggy.

"Wait, let me finish. No matter what Doug has done, you're still Finn's robot and—"

"I know, Abigail, but—" said Foggy.

"Will you stop being such a robot?" said Abigail, shaking Foggy by the shoulders. "I know human emotion is hard for you to understand, but Finn really cares and—"

"Yes, I comprehend, Abigail," said Foggy. "Sometimes people's actions don't actually express how they feel inside because they don't understand how they feel inside. So they fight, argue, or, I don't know, split up for no good reason and go their separate ways on planets doomed to explode."

"Oh, yeah," said Abigail. "That's basically

what I was going to say."

"And I was going to say we better get out of here, because one of those giants is stomping this way," said Foggy.

Foggy grabbed hold of Abigail and flew her back to the edge of the forest. They watched one of the brutes rip a tree straight out of the ground and carry it back to the ravine. The others joined him, and within a couple of minutes, they had uprooted more than a dozen trees.

"Can you see what they're doing with them,

Foggy?" asked Abigail.

Foggy could see the big aliens lashing the trees together and laying them across the chasm.

"It appears they've built some sort of bridge," said Foggy. "That's ironic. Oh, um, this is bad."

"What is it, Foggy?"

"Finn and Vale have now walked to the middle of that bridge. And, oh my goodness. No, they can't. I have to stop them!"

Foggy leapt off the branch and rocketed off into the sky. Through the smoke, Abigail couldn't see where he was going or what was happening out there with Finn and Vale. But whatever it was, she could tell it wasn't good.

Chapter Eleven
A Bunny with a Plan

Abigail raced back through the woods and found the clearing where the bunny and Elias were working. The death bunny had chopped down dozens of branches, kicking and biting them off trees.

Elias, for his part, was in the zone. Using vines from the forest, he'd tied the branches together. To Abigail, it still looked like a big pile of sticks that might be good for a campfire, but not much else. Elias was crouched down, working furiously.

"Um, Elias?" said Abigail. She stood over him. "Please tell me you have good news."

"Almost finished," he said without looking up.

"Because Doug has brainwashed Finn and Vale, and Foggy just shot off into the sky. So I really want some good news."

"I told you they'd been Doug'd," said the bunny, landing next to Abigail. He held two branches in his paws. "Doug did the same thing to a lot of my family. He convinced them they wanted to live somewhere else with a beach. We need to leave. Now!"

"How come you weren't brainwashed?" Abigail asked.

The bunny tapped his head.

"Nothing gets in here!" he said. Abigail could believe that.

"Okay, finished!" shouted Elias. "Bunny! You grab that stick there and walk away from me."

The bunny picked up a branch and pulled. The entire pile unfolded into what looked like a long, thin net. Elias looked at Abigail and smiled.

"It's a rope ladder!" he said. "See, the branches are what you grab on to, and the vines are the rope. It should be long enough to get us down to the ship. These branches are all from live trees, so they should be wet enough to not burn. AND—"

Elias picked up a handful of leaves.

"I've also rubbed the oils from these leaves into the branches, to make them extra fire-proof."

Elias beamed. He held up one of the vines to show Abigail how he'd tied off little looped knots. They looked like the bunny ears you make when you tie your shoes.

Abigail wasn't sure what to say.

"What are those for?" She pointed at one of the knots.

"So glad you asked!" said Elias. "They're super cool." Elias picked up a handful of small twigs.

"Anytime you see a crack or hole in the rock wall, you can slip one of these twigs through the hoops and pin the vines to the wall. It will help keep the ladder in place as you climb down."

"Me?" asked Abigail. "As I climb down?"

"No, not you specifically," said Elias. "I just mean 'you' like you or me or the bunny. One of us, any of us."

Abigail looked at him like he was crazy.

"You want us to climb into a lava pit?" asked Abigail.

"You're missing the point," said Elias. "The hoops are the best part. They're so we don't fall off the ladder."

Even as he was saying it, Elias had begun to realize the problem with his plan. No one would actually want to climb down a ladder into the molten center of an exploding planet.

"Forget it," said Elias. "We're doomed."

He sat down on a log, and the bunny sat next to him.

"Yep! We are," said the bunny. "But at least Doug is, too!"

Abigail was fed up with the situation.

"Why is that a good thing?!" she yelled. "Why did you blow up a planet, just to spite someone you don't like? How does that make you any better?"

Abigail paced around the clearing.

"And how did you do it, anyway? You're just a bunny. How does a bunny become a planet destroyer?"

"*Just* a bunny!" said the bunny, indignant. "I'll have you know only a bunny could do what I did."

Like a bank robber who'd been caught red-handed, the bunny was all too happy to tell Abigail and Elias how he'd blown up the planet.

"Listen to this!" said the bunny. "The planet's core is an ocean of white-hot magma. I know that because I like to dig, and I've dug farther than any bunny ever. So that magma, it's liquid rock, right? It runs through the entire planet through a series of underground tunnels and rivers. It heats the entire world! It provides steam to the hot springs, and minerals to the soil for the jungle plants. Every living being on the planet owes its life to the magma."

"Speed it up, Bunny," said Abigail.

"Like I said, I'm not just good at chopping down branches. I'm a world-class burrower. So over many weeks, I dug and dug and dug, far away from Doug and his Dougy brain. Eventually, I found the mouth of one of those magma rivers. I kicked and dug (no pun intended) until I'd piled up enough dirt and rock, cutting off that river of magma. Completely closed it off."

"And then you did that again and again, until no lava flowed out," said Elias. He stood up.

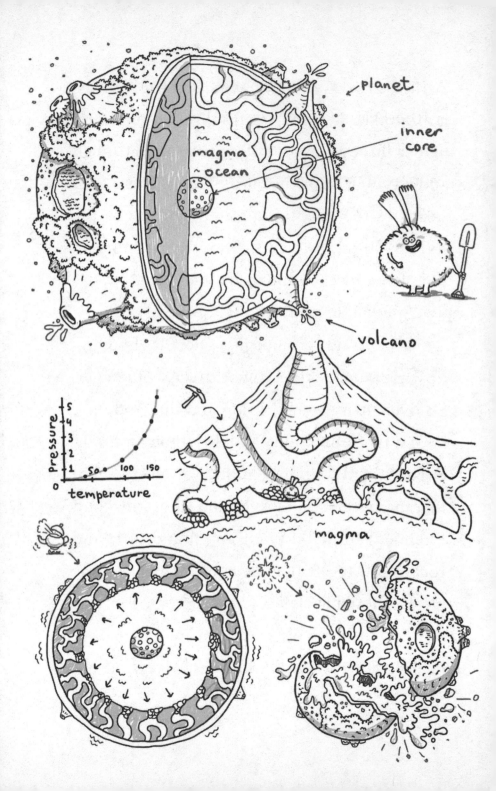

planet

inner core

magma ocean

volcano

magma

temperature

pressure

"And once all that magma built up in the center, the heat and the pressure became way too high. The steam generated by that magma had nowhere to go. So it exploded!"

"Co. Co. Nutted," said the bunny.

"It's actually kind of genius," said Elias. But Abigail wasn't listening. She was rolling up Elias's ladder.

"Okay, Bunny," she said. "March."

"Where are we going?" The bunny looked around, confused.

"You're going to show us how you got down there. Then we're going down and we're fixing this once and for all."

The bunny looked at Elias, shocked.

"She's the captain," said Elias, picking up one end of the ladder.

Chapter Twelve
The End Is Nearish

Finn balanced on the edge of the bridge that the giant aliens had just built. He looked down into the ravine. The planet was breaking apart. The bridge was shaking along with the planet. It was like standing on a seesaw during an earthquake.

Their ship was down there, in the ravine. It was made to withstand extreme temperatures, and it was still in one piece. It had rolled onto its side and landed on a shelf of rock. Beneath that shelf was a lake of molten lava.

Out of the corner of his eye, he could see Vale next to him. He looked as scared as Finn felt.

"And now," said Doug. "For a moment of incredible heroism. You will be spoken of for centuries to come. Finn and Vale, you are strangers to this world, but with this one selfless act you will become legends to our people. We are grateful to you, and we await your return."

Finn looked back at the edge of the cliff. A deep rumble came from below him. The planet had almost completely coconutted now. It was breaking apart. The quakes were so strong, even the giants looked like they might topple over. Finn couldn't quite remember how he and Vale had gotten onto the bridge. He looked over at his friend and saw that his head seemed to be glowing inside his helmet. Vale's eyes looked unfocused, like they weren't seeing what was in front of them.

"Why are we doing this?!" called Finn. "Why are you all standing over there while we are out in the middle of the chasm?"

"Because only you know how to fly the ship." Doug's words appeared in his head. "You have to be the ones to go get it."

Finn shook his head, trying to clear out Doug's words, but he couldn't. All he could picture was himself and Vale jumping off the bridge. They would land on the pod. They would fly the ship up and out of there. They would pick up the aliens and drink lemonade as they escaped. Why was it always lemonade? He didn't even like lemonade.

"Please hurry now," said Doug. "We have maybe six minutes left. But that's being generous."

It was all so overwhelming for Finn. The pictures in his head, the heat from the chasm, the smoke rising all around them. He and Vale held hands. Without saying a word, they listened to Doug's counting in their heads.

"Three . . . two . . . one."

They jumped.

The steam from the magma blew brutal

winds up at them. Their space suits became hotter and hotter as they plummeted. Finn squeezed Vale's hand even tighter. Vale's eyes were now focused, and terrified, looking back at Finn. There was nothing they could do. They had to hope they could land on the ship and get inside it.

But they weren't falling toward the ship. They were headed right for the lava!

Suddenly, a gust of wind knocked them sideways. They spun wildly. Finn couldn't tell which way was up.

It was just a few seconds before Finn realized they weren't falling anymore. They were headed toward a rocky ledge. And it wasn't the wind that had changed their direction. It was Foggy! The robot had grabbed Finn's left ankle and Vale's right elbow and was piloting them to safety.

When they landed, Finn hugged Foggy
hard.

"Thank you" was all he could say, he was
so out of breath. But Vale had recovered a little
more quickly.

"Wow, great work," he said to Foggy as

they high-fived. "You kept us from becoming doom doughnuts."

Finn grabbed Foggy. He needed to explain to the robot that Doug had messed with Vale's brain.

"You know," said Vale. "Because we would have been dunked into the lava. And that would have been our doom. Like if you dunked a doughnut. Into doom. Doom doughnuts. Think about it for a second. It works."

Finn laughed.

"Hey, you're back!" said Finn.

"Yep, totally un-Doug'd!" laughed Vale.

"Foggy, I'm so sorry," said Finn. "I—I couldn't think straight. Doug had—"

"I know," said Foggy. "The bunny told us you'd been Doug'd. And I know your next question, too. I left Abigail and Elias up in the forest. Elias was building something to help get us out of here. But now that we're here, we should be able to just get in the ship and fly to them."

"One problem," said Vale. "Actually, three problems. Three very large, very angry problems."

Vale pointed up. The giant aliens were quickly climbing down the rock face. And they did not look happy.

Chapter Thirteen
Vale to the Rescue

"Leave them to me," said Vale, ready to confront the aliens. "I'm the sergeant-at-arms."

"What are you talking about?" said Finn. "How are we going to leave three massive aliens to you?"

"Yeah, good call," said Vale. "I'm glad you said that. Any other plans?"

"Foggy. Foggy, can you hear me?"

Finn could hear a familiar voice, but he couldn't see who was speaking.

"Is that Abigail?" asked Finn.

"Can she talk to us like Doug now?!" cried Vale. "Get out of my head, Abigail!"

"No, chuckleheads," said Abigail. "I'm over here. To your left."

Finn could see the hand of Abigail's space suit waving from a hole in the rock. It went back into the wall, and then Abigail's face poked out.

"We followed one of the tunnels the bunny dug and came out down here. Long story. But the point is that we need to make a big hole just to the left of us. There's a lava river there that the bunny blocked up. If we can move the rocks out of the way, then maybe the lava can flow again and the planet will heal. Or at the very least, it can explode a little slower."

CRASH! One of the giant aliens landed on the shelf of rock where Finn, Vale, and Foggy stood. *CRASH.* The second landed just behind him. The shelf cracked. The third alien was almost there. Finn wasn't sure the shelf would hold all of them.

"We've got a different kind of problem out here," said Finn. The first giant alien lifted up an enormous foot and brought it crashing down, narrowly missing Finn, who rolled out of the way. The rock shelf cracked even further. Steam burst through.

"Cut it out, big guy!" said Finn. "Or you're going to send us all into the lava."

BOOM. The third giant alien landed on the shelf. The explorers could feel the whole thing start to tip.

"Leave them to me," said Vale.

"Again?" said Finn. "We've been through this, Vale."

"No, I'm serious. This time I got it."

Vale ran over to the first big alien and shouted: "ALKFJALKFJAFKJALKFJ!"

The three aliens shrieked, and two of them began climbing hurriedly back up the cliff.

"What did you just say to them?" asked Finn.

"I told them there were spiders down here," said Vale. "Those guys are such chickens."

ROOOAAARRR!

The third alien lifted up its right foot and slammed it down, trying to stomp on Vale. Vale jumped out of the way. Apparently, this giant wasn't scared of spiders. Vale ran past where Abigail was hiding and started doing a little dance to make the alien angry.

"BOULRELANNFA," he yelled.

The alien roared again and kicked out at Vale, slamming its foot into the rock wall.

"What did he say?" asked Foggy.

Finn laughed.

"No idea, but if I had to guess, he just called that alien a chucklehead."

A huge hole opened up where the giant

had kicked the wall, and a blast of steam from the lava inside shot out. Finn, Vale, and Foggy jumped out of the way as lava began to pour out. Vale had tricked the aliens into making a hole in the rock wall!

"You did it, Vale!" said Abigail.

The bunny dug at the tunnel entrance, making it big enough for Abigail, Elias, and the furry alien to squeeze through and climb down to the rock shelf. Vale hugged his friends as they landed.

Finn could suddenly see a picture of Doug on the beach. Then Doug swimming. Then Doug surfing. He was a really terrible surfer.

"No, not now," said Finn, shaking his head.

"Look out!" yelled the bunny as the giant alien came running at them.

But Elias was ready. He flung one end of the ladder to Abigail, and they wrapped it around the alien's legs. The alien tripped and fell with an enormous crash.

"See, Elias?" said Abigail. "It's a net."

Elias shrugged. "The sign of a well-engineered tool is that it can be used for multiple purposes."

Abigail and Elias high-fived. They turned to Finn. But Finn wasn't celebrating.

His head was glowing red. "No, no, this can't be happening," he said.

Abigail grabbed hold of his shoulders. "Finn,

whatever Doug is saying, it doesn't matter," she said. "It's over now."

But Finn ignored her. His head glowed a brighter red. He turned away and ran over to the explorer pod. He jumped in and powered it on.

"Finn, no!" shouted Foggy, but Finn closed the hatch, locking himself in and Foggy out.

"AGAEFAFAOPIJAF," yelled Finn. And the explorer pod shot out of the ravine, up into the air, and over the cliff.

The ship and Finn were gone.

Chapter Fourteen
Doug Unplugged

The explorers all followed the bunny back through one of the tunnels it had dug. Abigail was the last in line. It was so dark, she could barely see Elias in front of her. Foggy, exhausted from flying around the planet, lit the way with a dim light from his chest. The poor robot was so tired, he couldn't even fly out of the ravine.

Abigail was in shock. They had come so far. They hadn't stopped the planet from splitting, but they had reopened the flow of lava so the planet could heal. They had even made it back to their ship and been ready to fly home to the *Marlowe*.

But then Finn ruined it. No, not Finn. Doug ruined it, by using Finn to steal their pod.

Finally, they climbed out of the bunny's tunnel. They were near the edge of the forest. They collapsed, too tired and too sad to move.

Vale looked up. The explorer pod was disappearing into the upper atmosphere of the planet.

"There he goes," said Vale. "I can't believe Finn did that."

No one said anything. No one could find the words to make things better.

"Did what?" said a voice from behind them. "Saved everybody? Yeah, Finn is such a chuckle-head."

The explorers all looked up. There was Finn, walking toward them, smiling.

"What the—?!" said Elias. He stood up and grabbed a small stick. "Stay back, Finn! We know you're controlled by Doug!"

Finn put his hands in the air like he was surrendering.

"It's me, Elias, I swear," he said. "I was just pretending to let Doug take control of me. You guys saw how powerful he is. I knew that he would never let us get off the planet. He would just take control of me, or one of you. I had to trick him first, before he could trick us."

"What a great trick!" said Vale. "You gave him our only way off this planet and left us behind to climb through one of the bunny's gross tunnels! You really showed Doug!"

Finn laughed. "Don't you see? I knew Doug would leave me behind. I kept seeing myself fly away with the aliens. But I knew it was fake. He always showed me drinking lemonade, and I *hate* lemonade. So I knew that would never happen, and he'd leave all of us here. A guy like that doesn't think of anyone but himself. So I pretended I was following his instructions and stole the pod."

"But your head was red," said Abigail.

"Yeah," said Finn. "Doug was really trying. It took everything I had to resist."

"Yeah," said Vale. "That's really cool and everything, Finn, but what about our pod?"

"Oh, I preprogrammed its destination. I noticed one of the moons of this planet as we were flying in. It was bright blue."

The bunny laughed.

"That thing is basically just a giant chunk of ice," he said.

"Exactly," said Finn. "So I set the pod to fly to that moon. The aliens have no idea how to fly the ship. That's why they needed me and Vale in the first place. So Doug is officially stranded."

"Now he's on a floating iceberg in space," said Abigail. "And once we alert the *Marlowe*, they can just autopilot the pod, without Doug, back to the space station. Not bad, Caspian."

Finn looked down.

"I'm sorry I betrayed you guys," he said.

"Forget about it," said Abigail. "Someone was literally controlling your mind."

"No, before that," said Finn. "We're an awesome team. And we're an awesome team because we're all good at what we do. I should have listened to you, Abigail."

"Yep!" said Abigail. "Everyone remember this day. Finn Caspian finally admitted he needs to listen to me."

The explorers all laughed. Finn blushed.

"Forget about it," said Abigail. "You figured it out, and you saved the day. So I guess we can forgive you."

"Actually, I saved the day," said Vale. "I got the lava river flowing again."

"But it was my ladder net that kept that

giant from crushing us," said Elias. "So I think I saved the day."

Finn stepped between them.

"Actually, Abigail is the one who found the way to stop the planet from coconutting," said Finn. "Great work, Captain."

Chapter Fifteen
Home, Sweet Space Station

Elias tore out the walkie-talkie from his space suit. He did the same with each of the explorers. After about an hour of fiddling with them, he showed his friends what he'd built.

"Behold!" he said. "Super-Walkie-Talkie!"

Elias pressed a button on the clump of wires and fuses in his hand.

"There," he said. "The *Marlowe* ought to hear that."

Soon, they saw a dot appear in the planet's yellow sky. As a *Marlowe* rescue ship landed, the explorers all took turns hugging the bunny goodbye. The ship was unmanned, so Abigail got in and sat down in the pilot's seat. The explorers and Foggy followed and strapped in. The bunny waited outside to see them off.

"Are you sure you don't want to come with us?" said Elias.

"Nah," said the bunny. "I got stuff to do down here. Lots of trees to chop down, now that I'm a lumberjack, of course."

The bunny paused.

"And, you know," he said. "I thought I'd fix the place up a bit. Bring my family back."

"Okay, but one last thing," said Abigail. "Care to do the honors?"

The bunny laughed. He hopped over and jumped onto the big red launch button while Abigail pulled on the throttle.

"So that's how it works," said the bunny. He hopped back, the hatch closed, and the pod took off. It was headed home.

The trip to the *Marlowe* was short, but it felt like forever. When the pod's doors finally opened inside the docking bay, the kids all hopped out. Before they could even set foot into the hallway of the *Marlowe*, their parents rushed at them.

"What happened?" asked Finn's mother, captain and head astronaut of the *Marlowe*. She grabbed Finn's hands and stared into his eyes. "You were supposed to go to a different planet and then suddenly you disappeared and then we saw the planet explode!"

"Technically, it coconutted," said Vale. His father had him in a giant bear hug. "Kind of like what's going to happen to me in a second."

Finn's mother looked at Vale like he had seven heads. But before Finn could say anything, she was hugging him, too. She placed a giant kiss on the glass of his helmet. Finn's little sister, Paige, came up and pinched him on his arm.

"Ow!" said Finn. "What was that for?"

"Next time, it's my turn," said Paige. "You always get all the fun."

"It wasn't really fun," said Abigail, who was holding her dad's hand. "It was mostly exhausting."

"What are you talking about?" asked Elias. He turned to his parents. "Mom, Dad. This bunny and I made this awesome rope ladder. It had all these loops on it. It was so cool. I'll show you. Oh! And the whole planet exploded!"

"Actually, not the whole planet," said Captain Caspian. "Come on. We'll show you."

They all went to the map room, and Captain Caspian turned on the projector. She showed them a video of the bunny's planet. The lava that had rushed back into the ravine eventually cooled as it rose and fused the two halves of the planet back together.

"You guys did that," said Captain Caspian. "You should be proud. Job well done."

"It's not quite done," said Finn. "We should contact the bunny's family and let them know it's safe to return."

"Good idea," said Captain Caspian.

"And then, you know, there's Doug," said Finn. He was still embarrassed that he'd let

Doug take over his brain.

"I've already put that explorer pod on autopilot," said Finn's mother. "It should be here soon."

"With Doug on board?!" yelled Finn. "Oh no, Mom, you don't know what he's like! He can control us. It's not safe!"

Finn's mother smiled.

"No, he's not on board," she said. "He can stay on that moon for a while, until he cools off."

Finn laughed, and he caught Abigail's eye. She was laughing, too.

The four friends stepped out into the hall as their parents discussed what to do with Doug. The corridor was empty except for the kids and a small cleaner bot in the corner, scrubbing at a hardened pudding stain on the space station floor.

Elias pulled out his robot notebook.

"Look what I drew," he said. "I just did it really fast on the way back from the planet. It's a design for a new bunnybot!"

"Guys," said Finn. "I'm sorry to interrupt, Elias, but I have to say this. I know it was Doug who controlled me down there, but you guys are my best friends. I promise it'll never happen ammmffff."

Abigail covered Finn's mouth with her hand.

"I told you," said Abigail. "Forget it."

"I know, but I want to say that—ow!"

A spitball bounced off Finn's cheek. Vale smiled with a straw between his lips. "Okay, okay," said Finn. "I get it. Thanks, guys."

The four of them began walking toward their compartments so they could finally get some sleep.

Paige came running out of the map room.

"Hey! Where are you going?!" she yelled at them. "Are you going off on another adventure? You better not be going off on another adventure. Because I'm going with you on the next one. Do you hear me?"

"Not now," said Finn.

"Yeah," said Vale. "We've had enough tiny people bossing us around for one day."

Acknowledgments

This toy rocket, which has been built out of cardboard, duct tape, and flop sweat, would never have gotten off the ground without the help of a lot of amazing people who aren't me. I owe a deep gratitude to Joanna MacKenzie, Maria Barbo, and Camille Kellogg, who have all taught me a lot. Thanks also to Julie Shapiro for her early nudge, and to Ben Strouse, Chris Tarry, and David Kreizman of Gen-Z Media for being great copilots.

Many reading this may know that the characters in this book first came to life as a podcast. I would be a chucklehead not to say thank you to every parent and kid who has tuned in to the show over the years.

Finally, thanks to my first editor and toughest critic, my son Griffin. And thanks to his brother, the show's intern and wild card, Emerson.

And, as I say every day, special thanks to Maria Villanueva.

Blast off into more adventures, inspired by the award-winning kids' podcast!

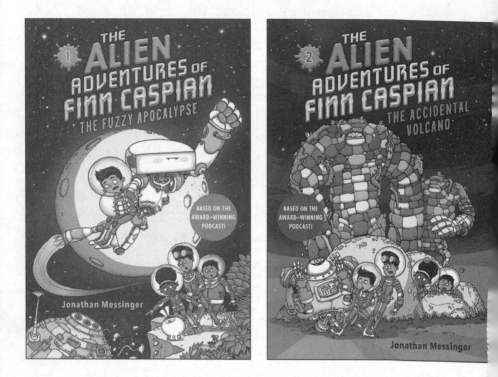

HARPER

An Imprint of HarperCollins*Publishers*

harpercollinschildrens.com